Rabbit's Story and *Teddy's Story* first published in 1988

This edition published in 1993 by Dean,
an imprint of Reed Consumer Books Ltd
Michelin House, 81 Fulham Road, London SW3 6RB
and Auckland, Melbourne, Singapore and Toronto

Text copyright © 1988 Rose Impey
Illustrations and design copyright © 1988 Sue Porter

ISBN 0 603 55124 6
A CIP catalogue record for this book is available at the British Library

Produced by Mandarin Offset
Printed in Hong Kong

Rabbit and Teddy Tales

Rose Impey & Sue Porter

RABBIT'S STORY

TEDDY'S STORY

DEAN

Rabbit's Story

Mummy, can we have a story?
What kind of story?
A story from the storybag.
All right, let's see who's inside tonight…

We'll call this 'Rabbit's Story'.

One moonlit night, very late, when all good
children were tucked up in bed, Rabbit was
fast asleep, dreaming rabbit dreams of crisp green
lettuce and juicy red carrots and young white turnips.
…But not everyone was tucked up in bed.

Not very far away, someone was wide awake and just coming out of her house. Cat walked down the road on soft, padded paws. She sniffed the air, looking for adventure.

Suddenly she saw something unusual.

A ladder was leaning against the wall and on the ground beside it was a sack. Now Cat was a curious creature, so she opened the sack. And what do you think she found inside? A mask, a torch and a stripy sweater. Cat dressed up and turned into a burglar.

Cat-burglar picked up the ladder and the sack and went to look for a house to burgle. Very soon she came to Rabbit's house. Rabbit had left his window open to let in a little fresh air. Cat-burglar leaned the ladder against the side of Rabbit's house and climbed up.

She turned on her torch and looked around.
'Rabbit's having a good dream. I'll steal that and take
it home for myself.' She crept inside and stole Rabbit's
dream. Then she climbed down, put it in her sack
and ran off home on her little padded paws.

Soon Rabbit woke up. He rubbed his eyes and hopped out of bed. 'What has happened to my dream?' he said. He saw the window wide open and the ladder outside. Then he knew what had happened.
He called out, 'Help! Help! Someone has stolen my dream.'

Well, who do you think was coming along the road just then?

A policeman!

'Now, now, what's all this noise? You'll wake everyone up, shouting like that,' he said. 'Someone has stolen my dream. I can't sleep without it,' said Rabbit. 'I want it back.' And he began to cry. 'You had better come with me,' said the kind policeman.'We'll try and find your dream and the rascal who stole it.'

He looked around for some clues. Along the road were bits of lettuce and carrot tops. So the policeman followed the trail and Rabbit followed the policeman, picking up the lettuce and carrots and eating them as he went.

The trail led them to Cat's house. They could hear
Cat inside making a strange noise. 'M-m-miaow,
m-m-miaow!' It was a most unhappy cry.
The policeman knocked on the door. 'Rat-a-tat-tat.
Open up, Mistress Cat!'

Cat looked out of her bedroom window. She was tired and cross.

'What's all this noise?' asked the policeman.

'I can't get to sleep. It's this stupid dream,' said Cat. 'It's giving me stomach ache. I want to dream about fish and milk and tasty little flies. I've never had such a bad night's sleep. You can have your silly old dream.' And she threw down the sack.

'Perhaps that will teach you a lesson, you bad Cat,' said the policeman. 'Come along, Rabbit. It's time to go home.'

But Rabbit had eaten so much on the way that he was full up and fast asleep on Cat's doorstep.
'Now how am I going to get you home?' thought the policeman.
Coming down the road, clipetty-clop, clipetty-clop, was a farmer with his horse and cart, on the way to market.

'Can you help me to take this young Rabbit home?' asked the policeman. And they lifted Rabbit into the cart.

The sun was beginning to rise as they jogged along the road. The policeman yawned. 'I'm ready for a good day's sleep,' he said, 'and a dream about a soft-boiled egg, a piece of toast and marmalade and a nice cup of tea.'

Have a good dream.

Teddy's Story

Grandma, can we have a story?
   What kind of story?
A story from the storybag.
   All right, let's see who's inside today…

We'll call this 'Teddy's Story'.

One fine day, not so very long ago, a Teddy set out to see the world. He wore a velvet cloak and a golden crown which shone in the sun.
He looked like a brave prince, but he wasn't.
Teddy loved to dress up and pretend. Sometimes this got him into trouble.

As he walked along, Teddy whistled a tune.
He didn't notice that 'someone' was hiding behind a tree, watching him.

It was a wicked Witch and if there ever was
a wicked Witch it was this one.
'Ha ha ha ha! A handsome prince,' she said.
'Exactly what I'm looking for.'

'But I'm not really a prince,' said Teddy.
'You look like a prince to me,' said the Witch.
'I shall put you under a spell and lock you up for
a hundred years, or more if I feel like it.'
Without another word, she carried him away.

They flew on the wind until they came to a tall castle, hidden deep in the dark, dark woods. The witch took Teddy to the very top of the castle and locked him in.

Now Teddy was in real trouble. There was no way to escape. He could only wave for help and hope someone might pass by and see him.

Quite by chance, someone did pass by. Doll was on the way to visit her grandma, who lived on the edge of the dark, dark woods.

When she saw Teddy waving for help, Doll began to search for a way in to rescue him. Soon she found a hole leading down into a tunnel. It was slimy and grimy underground, but Doll kept on bravely to the end of the tunnel where she found a door. Opening it a crack, Doll slipped through and found herself in the Witch's kitchen.

The Witch was stirring a cauldron, which bubbled like thick porridge on the stove. She was chanting a spell,

Eye of bat, tooth of rat,
Hair of dog, tusk of hog,
Unicorn's horn, Quails tail,
Season it all with shells of snail.

As doll crept past, she took one of the Witch's eggs out of a box on the table. 'Teddy might be hungry,' she thought. Then she raced up the steep stairs to the very top of the castle.

When Doll unlocked the door, she found Teddy
lying asleep on the bed, dreaming. She tiptoed
across the room and kissed him on the end of
his nose.
'Who are you?' said Teddy, waking up and blushing.

But there was no time for Doll to explain.
Already they could hear the Witch's hard little
feet climbing the stone staircase. Now they were
both in trouble.
'Oh dear,' said Teddy, 'what are we going to do?'
Doll reached in her pocket and took out the egg.

Doll rolled the egg towards the door. She hoped the Witch might trip over it and give them a chance to escape. But this was a magic egg. As it rolled, it grew bigger and bigger. When it reached the door it split in two with a loud, 'Craaacck!'

Out leaped a Monster with needle-sharp teeth. The Monster opened his mouth wide and roared. 'HHRRRAAARRGHGH!' The whole castle shook.

The Witch was terrified. She ran downstairs and kept on running until she was very far away.

At first Doll and Teddy were frightened too. But Monster told them how the wicked Witch had captured him many years ago and trapped him inside the egg.

'You helped me to escape,' he told Doll.
'What can I do for you?'
'Would you take us home?' said Doll. 'My
grandma will have tea ready.' And Doll and
Teddy climbed onto Monster's back.

As they sailed over the dark, dark woods
towards her grandma's house, Doll said to Teddy,
'Wait till my grandma sees that I've brought a
brave and handsome prince to tea.'
Teddy smiled. He felt like a handsome prince.
'You may kiss my paw,' he said. But Doll kissed
his nose instead.